To Mom and Dad, whose love and encouragement
have rained down in my life like a flood.
C.B.

> "Love the Lord your God with all your heart and with all
> your soul and with all your strength and with all your
> mind,' and, 'Love your neighbor as yourself.'"
>
> LUKE 10:27

ZONDERKIDZ

Get Me to the Ark on Time
Copyright © 2010 by Cuyler Black

Requests for information should be addressed to:

Zonderkidz, Grand Rapids, Michigan 49530

Library of Congress Cataloging-in-Publication Data

Black, Cuyler.
  Get me to the ark on time / written by Cuyler Black.
     p.   cm.
     Summary: A flamingo, continually interrupted by an anteater, tells a story
of two giraffes on Noah's ark who attempt to rescue a pair of turtles in danger
of being trapped outside as the waters rise.
     ISBN 978-0-310-71633-4
     1. Animals—Fiction. 2. Noah's ark—Fiction. 3 Deluge—Fiction. 4. Christian
life—Fiction. 5. Humorous stories.] I. Title.
PZ7.B556Get2010
[E]—dc22   2008048894

All Scripture quotations unless otherwise noted are taken from the *Holy Bible, New
International Version*®. NIV®. Copyright © 1973, 1978, 1984 by International Bible
Society. Used by permission of Zondervan. All rights reserved.

Editor: Mary Hassinger
Art direction and design: Kris Nelson

Printed in China

Get Me to the Ark on Time

Written & Illustrated by Cuyler Black

ZONDERk!dz

ZONDERVAN.com/
AUTHORTRACKER
follow your favorite authors

God sent two of every kind: elephants... tigers... bats... snakes... kangaroos... eagles... butterflies... crocodiles... polar bears... flamingos... raccoons...

The lion made sure that he and his mate were the first to get on board. He also insisted that they would be the first to get off the boat when it found dry land.

The giraffes had the hardest time on the ark. Their legs and necks were so long that they just couldn't get comfortable.

That does NOT look relaxing.

The other animals laughed at the giraffes' efforts. This hurt the giraffes' feelings more than the ceiling hurt their heads.

– Ow!

There was a rescue!

Check out Cuyler Black's other funny books and products!

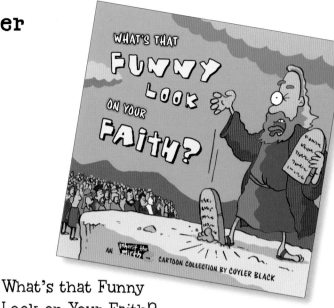

The Goat of Many Colors
978-0-310-71634-4

A creative twist on the story of Joseph and the coat of many colors. Children will learn that God gives each of us special gifts.

What's that Funny Look on Your Faith?
978-0-310-81397-2

A Far Side-type comic romp through the Bible. Young and old will find it laugh-out-loud funny and a great way to present faith to those who think believers need to "lighten up!"

Send-A-Laugh Postcards
- Church Life Cartoon Postcards
- Special Occasion Cartoon Postcards
- Old Testament Cartoon Postcards
- New Testament Cartoon Postcards

Each of these 32-page books includes 30 postcards that can be torn out and mailed. Each of the 120 original cartoons stand alone as a lighter, humorous look at faith while keeping a respectful tone.

See more Cuyler Black creations at Inheritthemirth.com